Hidden Talent

Contents

Chapter 1

The Idea

Becks ran up to Max in the playground, her eyes

sparkling with excitement.

"Max!" she yelled. "Have you heard the news?

The school talent show is open for entries!"

Comhairle Contae
Átha Cliath Theas
South Dublin County Council

Hidden
Talent

by Cath Jones and Anne Defreville

W
FRANKLIN WATTS
LONDON•SYDNEY

Max stared at Becks in surprise.

"What's so exciting about that?" she asked.

"Meghan Munroe ..." Becks said mysteriously.

Max shrugged her shoulders. "What about her?"

Becks began to bounce up and down on the spot.

"You know ... Meghan Munroe ... she judges that

show on the telly. It's my absolute and complete

favourite show of all time. I've wanted to go on it

since I was four years old!"

"Yeah, I know that."

"Well, I've heard that she's coming to judge here,"

Becks said. "This is our chance to be famous!

When we win ..."

"We?" interrupted Max, with a sinking feeling.

Becks nodded. "You, me, Ruby, Ronnie and Austen
are going to form a dance crew!" Her voice tailed
off. "Why are you looking at me like that, Max?"
Max laughed. "I can't help it, Becks. You always
believe we can do anything and you're so
enthusiastic but ..."
"But what?" asked Becks.

Max didn't want to disappoint her best friend
but the very idea of standing on a stage made her
want to crawl into the nearest hole and hide.
She took a deep breath. "I don't want to be in
a crew."

Becks stopped jumping up and down and stared at
her friend. "But you're such a brilliant dancer ..."

"That's when it's just you and me together. I don't want to stand up on stage with hundreds of people staring at me."

"But you make up your own routines, you can do back flips ..."

"Nope." Max folded her arms and shook her head. "It doesn't matter what you say. I'm not going to be in a crew."

Becks looked down, defeat written all over her face. "But we *need* you, Max," she pleaded.

Chapter 2

The Crew

At home time, Becks, Ruby, Ronnie and Austen were all waiting for Max at the school gate.

"We've made a decision," Ruby said.

"Right?" Max said uneasily.

"The five of us are going to be the best crew ever," Becks said.

Max frowned. "I told you I don't want to be in a crew."

Everyone laughed. "You are not *in* the crew."

Ronnie held up a hand for silence.

"You are an amazing dancer – you've definitely got the moves but ..." he paused for dramatic effect,

"... you're too shy to show the world."

Max looked at Ronnie suspiciously. "Ye-ss?"

Austen grinned. "Well, you know what a show-off
Ronnie is and the rest of us are just the same,
so we'll go on stage and you'll be the mysterious
one that no one ever sees. You'll just teach us what
to do."

A smile spread across Max's face. "Deal," she said.

On Monday, the crew met properly for the first time at Ruby's house.

"I made up a new routine at the weekend," Max said, shyly, taking out her tablet. "Mum filmed me – do you want to see it?"

"Yes!" Becks made to grab Max's tablet.

Max held it above her head. "I'll only let you see it if you promise not to say anything mean."

"We promise," they all said.

Max felt nervous, but she was sure that her new routine was good, and so she took a deep breath and switched on her tablet. Becks, Ruby, Austen and Ronnie watched intently. Finally, the dance ended. No one made a sound. Max stared at their faces and her stomach twisted into a knot.

Becks looked at Max. "I can't believe that was you!"

Max shifted in her seat uneasily.

"What did you think?"

"Wow," mouthed Becks.

"Genius," said Austen.

Ruby just stared, amazed.

A wave of relief flooded over Max. "You liked it!"

"Can you show us how it's done?" asked Ronnie,

"but slowly!"

"Well, if you're sure ..." said Max.

On Tuesday, the crew met for their first practice. After an hour, they fell on to the sofa, exhausted. "You've got more talent than all of us put together," Becks said. "I wish you'd be in the crew."

Max twisted the bottom of her T-shirt uncomfortably and shook her head. "I love doing this stuff with you guys and sometimes I do wish I could be more like you, but I just can't."

"So what are we going to call our crew?" said Austen.
"How about 'Hidden Talent'?" said Becks. "Get it? Max is our hidden talent!"
"Brilliant!" agreed Ronnie and the others, and Max smiled at her friends.

Chapter 3

Getting to the Show

The next two weeks whizzed by in a blur of energetic rehearsals. *Hidden Talent* met at each other's houses three times a week in the evenings, and for two hours each Saturday and Sunday.

They practised at home
in front of the mirror

... in front of
their parents

... and even in front
of their pets.

Now, it hardly seemed possible, but in less than
a quarter of an hour, the talent show would begin.

Max had almost reached the hall when she spotted it – parked in the middle of the car park was a sleek, red sports car. Tinted windows hid the interior from the curious gazes of passers-by. The personalised number plate, MEG 1X, left Max in no doubt as to who owned the car. She let out a tiny yelp. The rumours were true – Meghan Munroe was here! Becks would be over the moon with excitement.

A SOLD OUT sticker was stuck across the hall's main entrance door. That meant 250 people would be watching *Hidden Talent* perform her routine. A tingle of excitement swept through Max.

17

Max decided to sit at the very back of the hall.
She perched on a table and flicked through
the programme. She didn't really need to read it,
she knew *Hidden Talent* was first on stage.
Seeing their name in print made it all feel so real.

Then the lights dimmed.
A murmur of
whispered anticipation
rippled through the hall.

Then nothing.
The curtain didn't go up.
There was no music.

Suddenly, a teacher emerged from behind
the curtain and called to Mrs Chen,
the headteacher. With a worried glance
around the hall, Mrs Chen hurried backstage.

Chapter 4

Disaster!

A minute or so later, the hall lights went back up and Mrs Chen walked on to the stage. A hush fell across the hall.

"I have an announcement to make," said Mrs Chen, her voice wavering slightly. "There has been an accident and unfortunately, *Hidden Talent* will no longer be opening the show as ..."

Mrs Chen's voice was drowned out as everyone started talking at the same time.

Max listened in disbelief and a wave of panic washed over her. She stood up and sprinted towards the backstage area.

The first thing Max saw backstage was Becks's tear-stained face. Becks was sitting on the floor with a first-aider crouched down in front of her, examining her swollen ankle.

When Becks spotted Max, she cried even harder. "Oh Max!" she sobbed. "I tripped on the steps and they think I've twisted my ankle. I can't put any weight on it ..." Her voice trailed off.

Max felt hollow inside. This was the end. All their dreams shattered in an instant – the rehearsing and practising, all for nothing.

Becks sobbed even louder. "If *Hidden Talent* doesn't go on within the next ten minutes, we'll be disqualified."

Max went pale. But she knew what she had to do.

Chapter 5

The Show Must Go On

Slowly, silently, the curtain rose. For a brief moment, both the stage and audience were in darkness. Other than a faint cough somewhere in the audience, the hall was totally quiet.

Without warning, a single spot light flicked on. Max gasped. She froze like a rabbit caught in a car's headlight. "How on Earth did I end up on this stage?" she thought. "Hundreds of people are watching me! Everyone in *Hidden Talent* is depending on me."

Her hands were sticky with sweat. She looked over to where Becks was sitting at the side of the stage. "You can do this," whispered Becks.

Ruby opened with a back flip. Max stiffened. She felt as though she were glued to the surface of the stage.

The music got louder as the drums started. Max gulped back the panic rising inside her. Ruby was already beginning to move around the stage, with Ronnie and Austen weaving around her.

Max fixed a smile on her face and began to move. All at once, she felt the excitement steal over her. Her fingers tingled and her heart thudded. "It's up to me now," she thought.

The audience seemed to disappear. Max didn't even have to think about the routine. She knew these moves so well she could do them in her sleep!

As the music finished, the audience leapt to their feet. A wave of cheering swept across the hall. A smile spread across Max's face. "This feels good," she thought.

Becks gave a thumbs-up sign, happy tears filling her eyes. "You did it," she mouthed.

Suddenly, the spotlight shifted away from the stage and on to the audience. It settled on the front row; Meghan Munroe was on her feet, clapping and cheering along with everyone else. *Hidden Talent* was getting a standing ovation from the whole crowd – even Meghan Munroe!

The hall thundered with the sound of stamping feet and the audience began to chant their name over and over again.

"HI-DDEN TA-LENT! HI-DDEN TA-LENT!"

Becks beamed at Max. "Go on," she said. "This is your moment."

Max bowed along with the rest of the crew.

The audience went wild.

Things to think about

1. Why do you think Max does not want to be in the dance crew?
2. Do you think that Max's friends know her well?
3. How can you tell that the talent show is important to the friends?
4. Why does Max end up taking part in the talent show after all?
5. How do you think Max and Becks felt at the end of the story?

Write it yourself

One of the themes in this story is friendship. Now try to write your own story with a similar theme.

Plan your story before you begin to write it.

Start off with a story map:

• a beginning to introduce the characters and where and when your story is set (the setting);

• a problem which the main characters will need to fix in the story;

• an ending where the problems are resolved.

Get writing! Try to include physical reactions to show how your characters feel, for example: Becks looked down; her stomach twisted into a knot; Max gulped etc.

Notes for parents and carers

Independent reading

The aim of independent reading is to read this book with ease. This series is designed to provide an opportunity for your child to read for pleasure and enjoyment. These notes are written for you to help your child make the most of this book.

About the book

When a school talent show is organised, Becks is desperate to enter. She wants to form a dance crew with her best friend, Max, but Max is too shy to take part even though she is a talented dancer. Her friends come up with a way to include Max in their plans, and she finally takes her chance to shine.

Before reading

Ask your child why they have selected this book. Look at the title and blurb together. What do they think it will be about? Do they think they will like it?

During reading

Encourage your child to read independently. If they get stuck on a longer word, remind them that they can find syllable chunks that can be sounded out from left to right. They can also read on in the sentence and think about what would make sense.

After reading

Support comprehension by talking about the story. What happened?
Then help your child think about the messages in the book that go beyond the story, using the questions on the page opposite. Give your child a chance to respond to the story, asking:
Did you enjoy the story and why? Who was your favourite character?
What was your favourite part? What did you expect to happen at the end?

Franklin Watts
First published in Great Britain in 2019
by The Watts Publishing Group

Series Editors: Jackie Hamley and Melanie Palmer
Series Advisors: Dr Sue Bodman and Glen Franklin
Series Designer: Peter Scoulding

A CIP catalogue record for this book is
available from the British Library.

ISBN 978 1 4451 6513 4 (hbk)
ISBN 978 1 4451 6514 1 (pbk)
ISBN 978 1 4451 6840 1 (library ebook)

Printed in China

Franklin Watts
An imprint of
Hachette Children's Group
Part of The Watts Publishing Group
Carmelite House
50 Victoria Embankment
London EC4Y 0DZ

An Hachette UK Company
www.hachette.co.uk

www.franklinwatts.co.uk

FSC
www.fsc.org
MIX
Paper from
responsible sources
FSC® C104740